R0085489706

BAGDASARIAN
PRODUCTIONS

ALVINNN!!! AND THE CHIPMUNKS™

The Campout Challenge

based on the screenplay "Kickin' It Old School"
written by Janice Karman
adapted by Lauren Forte

Ready-to-Read

Simon Spotlight
New York   London   Toronto   Sydney   New Delhi

SIMON SPOTLIGHT
An imprint of Simon & Schuster Children's Publishing Division
1230 Avenue of the Americas, New York, New York 10020
This Simon Spotlight edition December 2017
Alvin and The Chipmunks, The Chipettes and Characters TM & © 2017 Bagdasarian
Productions, LLC. All Rights Reserved. Agent: PGS USA.
For information about special discounts for bulk purchases, please contact
Simon & Schuster Special Sales at 1-866-506-1949 or business@simonandschuster.com.
Manufactured in the United States of America 1117 LAK
10 9 8 7 6 5 4 3 2 1
ISBN 978-1-5344-0932-3 (hc)
ISBN 978-1-5344-0931-6 (pbk)
ISBN 978-1-5344-0933-0 (eBook)

"Guys, I can't wait to start our
weekend retreat in the great
outdoors," Dave called from
the front seat.

The boys didn't even look up
from their games.

"I'm bored," Alvin complained.

"It will be good to spend quality
time together," Dave responded,
"without any . . . distractions."

"Oh no! My game shut down!"
Alvin cried.
"Mine too!" Simon chimed in.
"Aw, drat!" added Theodore.
"Oh, look!" Dave said as he got
out of the car. "We're here!"

But when they checked the cabin,
it was not in good shape.
"WHAT?" Dave asked, surprised.
"I knew it would be rustic,
but everything looks broken.
Oh well. We'll make it work."

"Wait," said Alvin in a panic.
"No cell service, no electricity?
All we'll have is . . . us!"
He couldn't believe it.

In a last effort Alvin ran outside
and climbed a tree.
He held his phone out to see
if he could get cell service.
"Anything?" Simon yelled up.
"No bars," Alvin said sadly.

"Come on, guys," Dave said.
"You can exist without
technology for two days."
The boys weren't buying it.

That night Dave made a campfire.
"Why don't I tell a scary story?"
he suggested.
"Sure," the boys agreed, still sad.
"Um . . . okay. A long time ago when
I was a young lad," Dave whispered.

"I lived in a house that was definitely haunted," he finished.

"That's it?" asked Alvin.

"I'm going to bed," said Simon.

"Sleep? After that bone-chilling horror story?" Alvin kidded.

Dave stayed by the fire to think.

The next morning Dave was filled
with energy and fresh ideas.
"Okay, guys. Wake up!
We're going on a hike!" he shouted.
Grumbling, they got out of bed.

"I camped a lot when I was an Eagle Scout," Dave said as they walked. "I learned such cool stuff. And your grandpa showed me how to tie ropes."

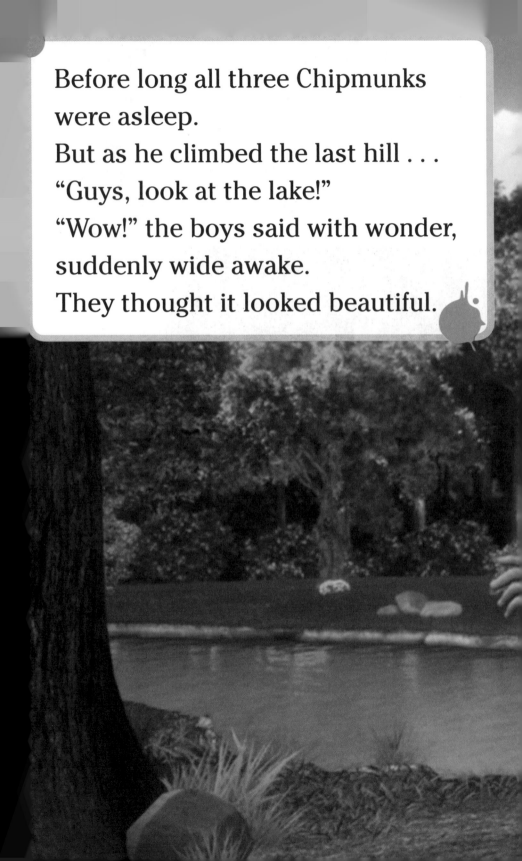

Before long all three Chipmunks
were asleep.
But as he climbed the last hill . . .
"Guys, look at the lake!"
"Wow!" the boys said with wonder,
suddenly wide awake.
They thought it looked beautiful.

"Let's go down there!" Alvin said.
Then he noticed Dave holding a rope.
"What's that for?" Alvin asked.
Dave smiled and put the boys down.

Dave quickly took off the clothes
that covered his bathing suit.
Then he swung out over the lake
on the rope swing.

"The water is great!
Come on in!" Dave urged.

The Chipmunks spent all morning
taking turns doing jumps, flips,
and dives off the rope.
They had a blast.

That afternoon Dave taught them which berries were okay to eat in the wild.

"Mmm," Theodore said happily.

When it grew dark, Dave showed
them how to make shadow puppets
with the flashlight.
Simon was great at it!

After that they chased fireflies
until they were all exhausted.

When they were finally relaxed and roasting marshmallows, Dave said, "I had so much fun today. Can I end the vacation with one last story?" The boys groaned. "Oh no . . ."

Alvin shook his head.
"Dave, I don't know how to say this,
but you're a terrible storyteller!"
Dave ignored Alvin as he helped the
Chipmunks into their hammocks.

"One more chance," Dave pleaded.
"So, as I said, my house was haunted.
It was near a forest, and an old,
angry man fell asleep in the
forest. And he became—Leaf-Man!"

"Lame," Alvin said right away.
Dave protested, "It's not—"
"Pretty lame," Theodore agreed.
Suddenly, the trees rustled.
"What's that?" Theodore cried.
"I'll check. Stay here," Dave warned.

Dave stepped into the bushes.
The boys heard loud grunting noises!
Then . . . out of nowhere . . .
"LEAF-MAN!" Dave hollered,
jumping from behind a tree.
"AHHHH!" screamed the boys.

Dave giggled. "Sorry, guys.
Still think Leaf-Man is lame?"
"Not funny," said Alvin as they
settled in Dave's lap.
"Let's just enjoy the rest of this
beautiful starry night," Dave said.

Dave handed them back their phones
on the ride home the next day.
"Pretty great time, huh?" he asked.
"It kills me to say this," Alvin replied,
"but yes—wait . . . yay!"
Their gadgets started beeping to life.
The boys were back to their old ways.

Dave was sitting at his computer
when Simon came in.

"Are you playing video games?"
Dave asked.

"Not exactly," Simon answered.
"Come out and see."

The boys had set up sleeping bags
in the backyard!
"Wow! This is great!" Dave said.
"Should I tell a story?"
The Chipmunks yelled, "Noooo!"